SECOND CHANCE

A Tale of Two Puppies

More praise for....

SECOND CHANCE
A Tale of Two Puppies

"Judy Masrud gives good insight into two different adoptions with a surprisingly happy ending!"
—GREG THOMPSON, HUMANE SOCIETY OF BARRON COUNTY, WI

"I have no doubt, Second Chance—A Tale of Two Puppies, will help place many more animals in good, loving homes."
—CHUCK TOURTILLOTT, DIRECTOR,
   HUMANE SOCIETY OF CASCADE CO., MT

"The stories of Boomer and Chance demonstrate the importance of having the time and understanding of what it takes to properly care for an animal and what can happen if you don't."
—JANELLE DIXON, EXEC. DIRECTOR,
   HUMANE SOCIETY FOR COMPANION ANIMALS, ST. PAUL, MN

"This is a book that you, your children, or your grandchildren can read, learn from, and enjoy."
—A.E. HORVATH, D.V.M.
   RIDGELAND VETERINARY SERVICE, RIDGELAND, WI

"...Explores the reality of pet ownership in a manner that children and adults can understand."
—SHERI MAREK, GOLDEN RETRIEVER RESCUE OF WISCONSIN

"... a very real account of two possible situations that illustrate the responsibility that goes along with dog ownership."
—DANETTE PHELPS, OBEDIENCE TRAINER,
   ON BEHALF OF MIDWEST BORDER COLLIE RESCUE

SECOND CHANCE

A Tale of Two Puppies

By Judy Masrud
Illustrated by Cathy Pool

BIRDSEED BOOKS
DALLAS, WI

ISBN-13: 978-0-9774142-0-8
ISBN-10: 0-9774142-0-5

Library of Congress Control Number: 2005909506

Book Cover & Interior Design by: www.book-cover-design.com
Cover Illustration by: Cathy Pool

Attention Schools, Book Clubs, and Professional Organizations:
Quantity discounts are available on bulk purchases of this book for
educational purposes. For information, please contact Birdseed
Books, 520 17th Street, Dallas, WI., 54733, Phone: 800-676-1160.

Judy Masrud is also the author/creator of Ringbound Reading™, a
comprehensive, hands-on phonics instruction curriculum, including
flash cards, games, and reinforcement projects. Non-consumable.

More information at www.birdseedbooksforkids.com

To every kid who wants a dog and promises to take care of it.

Andrew Wilson had spent most of his life trying to talk his parents into getting a dog. He'd read every book he could find on the subject, and after school, he could often be found walking Caesar or Cleo, the beagles who lived next door.

Every dog in the neighborhood loved Andrew and was always excited to see him. That, of course, was why he was the first to be called for dog sitting if one of the neighbors went on vacation. But still, Andrew knew, dog sitting just wasn't the same as having your own dog.

On his tenth birthday, Andrew awoke from the warm sunshine streaming in through his bedroom window. He rolled over, opened one eye, and saw light glinting off a big, shiny blue package on the floor in the middle of his room.

Throwing back the covers, Andrew jumped out of bed and grabbed the package, pulled off the curly red ribbons, and tore it open. He turned the box over and shook it, causing a sudden flurry of styrofoam peanuts. Andrew hardly noticed, for there in front of him lay a bright red collar, a leather leash, and a small yellow envelope. He grabbed the envelope and immediately ripped it open.

Dear Andrew,

    We've decided that it's time you get that puppy you've always wanted. You've proved yourself to be responsible. We're sure that any puppy would be lucky to have you as his best friend.

    Happy Birthday! We love you,

        Mom and Dad

    P.S. Plan on visiting the animal shelter this weekend. I've already called them. They have puppies!

"Yes!" Andrew yelled, hugging the note. Grabbing the leash and the collar, he jumped up and ran from his bedroom, nearly tripping over the rug in the hallway in his hurry to get down the stairs to the kitchen.

His parents, setting breakfast on the table, laughed as Andrew, still in his pajamas, raced into the room. His sandy brown hair fell across his eyes as he rushed over to his mom and dad and threw his arms around them.

"Thank you, thank you, THANK YOU!" he cried.

Welcome to the Franklin County Humane Society read the cheery white and blue sign in front of the animal shelter. As soon as Mrs. Wilson turned off the car, Andrew could hear the yips and squeals of excited puppies. He quickly opened the car door and ran toward the chain-link fence.

My very own puppy! he thought. *I can hardly believe it!*

Three months earlier, the puppies' mother, who was part Border collie, had been brought to the shelter as a stray. Her black fur was matted and crusted with dirt. Her paws were bleeding from cuts and sores. And, her belly was big. She was going to have puppies, very soon. Apparently, someone had dropped her off in the countryside, foolishly thinking that she could find her way to a good home.

The staff at the animal shelter had tenderly cared for her. They fed her, treated her wounds, bathed her, and brushed her. They also had made a bed of soft blankets in the corner room, where she would later deliver her litter of seven puppies. No one could be sure what would happen with her. She was a sweet and beautiful dog, but it was always easier to find homes for puppies than for adult dogs. So far, five of those puppies had been adopted.

"Oh, Mom, look at him," said Andrew, as he pointed at one of the puppies jumping up and down near the fence. "Look at his little white paws. I want to take him home!" He lifted the metal latch to open the gate and walked into the pen slowly, so he wouldn't frighten the puppies.

"We call that one Boomer," said one of the volunteers. "There's nothing shy about that little fella."

Andrew looked back at his mom, who had followed him into the pen, then slowly approached the puppy.

"Hi, Boomer," he said at last. He knelt down on the grass and waited until Boomer was ready to come to him. Soon the puppy was sniffing and licking Andrew's hand. Andrew then picked up the fluffy little pup and buried his face in its soft, thick fur. He looked up. "Isn't he cute, Mom?" he whispered.

Mrs. Wilson smiled. "He's *adorable*," she said, reaching out to pet the squealing, squirming puppy. Andrew set Boomer on the ground and watched him run and play.

"You can fill out an application for adoption if you'd like to take Boomer home," said the volunteer.

"Thanks," said Andrew. "That's *exactly* what I want to do!"

Later that day, another family, the Smiths, arrived at the animal shelter. Matt had been pestering his mom and dad nearly every day since he'd seen the TV series about the great hero dogs.

"Please, can I get a puppy?" he had begged. "Please, *please*?" Matt had been determined to have his own hero dog. When Mr. and Mrs. Smith had finally become tired of Matt's whining and begging, they gave in and promised him a puppy.

Matt saw the last of the litter, Chance, peeking out from behind the doghouse.

"Hi, Chance," he said. "You're gonna make a great hero dog!" Matt picked up the shy puppy while **Mrs. Smith** went into the office of the animal shelter to finish filling out the paperwork.

Don't forget, Andrew," said Mrs. Wilson when they arrived home. "Boomer is totally your responsibility. He will depend upon you for everything."

"I know, Mom," said Andrew. "I'll take good care of him, I promise." He looked at the list of puppy chores posted on the kitchen wall, then down at the little black ball of fur he was holding. "You're going to be a lot of work, Boomer," he said, then quickly added, "but you're *definitely* worth it!"

He set the puppy on the floor and put the new red collar around his neck. Then Andrew snapped a four-foot lead onto the collar and fastened the other end to a belt loop on his jeans.

Okay, Boomer," he said. "Now, wherever I go, you're gonna go too!"

At night, Andrew placed Boomer in a crate lined with a soft blanket beside his bed, where he would be safe.

During Boomer's first week home, Andrew took him to visit the veterinarian. There, Boomer got a thorough checkup and the shots he needed to keep him healthy. Andrew also bought flea and tick medication for Boomer and scheduled future visits for his booster shots.

You'll probably have many questions about your puppy, so choose a veterinarian who obviously enjoys working with people and dogs. Your vet will be able to tell you which shots your puppy needs, the type of food he should eat, and whether or not your puppy needs heartworm medication. Plan to take your puppy to the vet for regular checkups, for his shots, and later on, for neutering. Having your puppy neutered will mean that you will not be contributing to the problem of overpopulation among dogs. Ask your veterinarian for advice on when to have your puppy neutered.

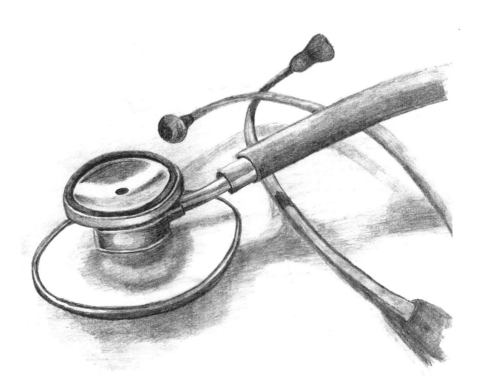

When Boomer was eleven weeks old, Andrew enrolled him in puppy kindergarten classes.

"You're going to go to school now, Boomer," he said. He held the puppy in one arm while opening the door of the training center with the other. As soon as Boomer saw the other puppies, he began barking and squirming to get free. Andrew set him on the floor, knelt down beside him, and snapped the leash onto his collar.

Boomer wasn't the only excited puppy. Eleven other puppies were in the class. All were about the same age and almost all of them were barking.

Puppy kindergarten helped Boomer get used to being around other people and other dogs.

Andrew learned how to teach basic obedience commands and how to get Boomer to pay better attention to him. Boomer learned to come, to sit, to lie down, to stay, and to walk beside Andrew without tugging on the leash.

Andrew took Boomer with him wherever he could. Boomer loved walking through the neighborhood and getting to know all the big kids, little kids, and grownups. He got used to the noise of bikes, scooters, skateboards, and motorcycles as they zoomed past. He loved getting rides in the car and going to Grandma's house. But the big, fenced-in dog park where he could run free and play with other dogs and puppies was his favorite place of all. He sometimes got treats. He *always* got lots of attention, and by the time he got home, he was *always* ready for a long nap.

att didn't know anything about socializing *his* pup—getting him used to being around people. Sadly, it was Chance who would suffer in the future because Matt hadn't taken the time to learn *anything* about puppies *before* he took a puppy home.

A puppy needs to spend lots of time around people, getting used to noises, and riding in the car. If you don't help him learn to feel secure while he is still young, he could develop fears that he may never outgrow.

One morning, Andrew was suddenly awakened by Boomer's wet tongue licking his face. "Oh, no," he groaned. "It can't be morning already." He rolled over and looked at the clock, then back at Boomer. The puppy was standing on his hind legs, struggling to climb onto the bed, his tail wagging wildly.

Andrew couldn't help smiling. "I guess no one's gonna be sleeping in around here," he said. He leaned over the edge of the bed and picked up the wiggly puppy. "I'm not sure I even need to have an alarm clock with you around," he said with a laugh.

Andrew got up and took Boomer downstairs. He set him on the floor while he went to get the puppy food ready. When he returned, Boomer was in the corner of the kitchen, going potty.

"Aach!" said Andrew, running to the puppy and scooping him up in his arms. He wasn't trying to frighten Boomer, just to startle him. He didn't say anything else, but quickly carried Boomer outside and set him down in the grass at the edge of the yard. Then he walked a few feet away and waited. This time, it was a little too late. Boomer walked around and sniffed the grass, but he didn't have to go potty anymore.

"Sorry, Boomer," Andrew said, picking him up. "That was my fault. I have to remember to take you out just as soon as you wake up in the morning."

When they returned to the house, Andrew cleaned up the corner and set Boomer's food bowl on the floor. "There you go, Boy," he said. Boomer eagerly gobbled down his food and then lapped up a long drink from his water bowl.

From then on, Andrew always made sure to get Boomer outdoors right after he woke up, after each meal, just before bedtime, and every few hours in between.

Each time Boomer went potty, Andrew said, "Good potty!" in a calm and pleasant voice. Boomer quickly learned that outdoors, rather than in the house, was the place to go to the bathroom. It wasn't long before he could be trusted to be off lead in the house.

Matt picked up his sweatshirt and sniffed the big, wet spot on the front.

"Oh great!" he shouted, throwing the shirt onto the pile of clothes lying on the floor. "What's is *the matter* with that puppy?! Yesterday it was my jeans," he mumbled. "Today it's my sweatshirt. Why does he have to pee on *everything I own*?"

Matt's father, coming down the hall, overheard him and poked his head in the doorway.

"Remember, Matt," he said, "we told you to housetrain that puppy. He can't learn it by himself, you know, and besides," he added, "it might help if you kept your clothes off the floor."

Matt sighed and plopped down onto the bed. *"Why me?* Why do I always have to be the one to take him out? I always have to do *everything!"* He looked out the window. "Do I have to take him out *even when it's raining*?" he whined.

"Matt, you're the one who wanted a puppy," his dad reminded him. "You said you were going to take care of him. You can't expect a puppy to just 'hold it' until the rain stops."

Matt grabbed Chance carelessly, ran downstairs, flung the door open, and set the puppy out on the wet doorstep. "Hurry up, Chance," he said, gruffly. Then he stepped inside the house, closed the door, and waited a few minutes.

Chance whined and shivered, huddling close to the back door to get out of the rain. He didn't know why Matt had left him out there all alone.

Eventually, the door was opened again and Chance ran inside. Matt dried him off, picked him up, and carried him to his bedroom. Then he dug through the pile of clothes to find a different shirt, and pulled it on over his head. While Matt wasn't looking, Chance went to the corner and peed on the rug.

Most puppies don't like to go to the bathroom in the same place they're going to want to walk or lie down or eat. If you keep a short lead on the puppy during the first few weeks after you get him home, and make sure to take him to the potty spot outdoors every couple hours, he'll eventually catch on. After that, when you do take him off lead in the house, don't give him the whole house at once. Expand his environment one room at a time. As he proves to be trustworthy, more room can be added and the potty breaks can gradually be farther apart. Remember: Be patient.

Playing with Boomer was a good way to teach him new commands, and Tag was Boomer's favorite game. Andrew knew that Boomer would want to follow him, so he used the game of Tag to work with Boomer on the Come command. "Come, Boomer, come!" he called, turning and running away from the excited puppy.

Boomer ran to Andrew. "Good Come," said Andrew, as he knelt down on the grass beside his puppy, hugging and petting him. "Okay, let's do it again!" Andrew turned and ran, calling Boomer again.

When Andrew's friends came to play, they helped him play a game of recall with Boomer. They would all stand in a big circle with the puppy standing next to one of them. Then they would take turns calling Boomer and coaxing him to come to them. Boomer was having tons of fun. He was getting lots of attention and exercise and learning to come when called.

"Mom, have you seen Chance?" called Matt. "I've hunted *everywhere*!" He looked behind the sofa, behind the door, and checked the bedrooms a second time.

"No, I haven't seen him," she answered. "Try checking outdoors, though, in case someone let him out."

Matt stood on the porch in his stocking feet. "Come, Chance, come Chance," he called, but still, he couldn't see the puppy anywhere. When he was just about to give up and look in the house again, Chance came bounding up the driveway.

"Chance, where *were* you?!" Matt yelled. "Don't you *ever* leave home again, you *bad puppy*! I've been looking all over for you!"

Chance ran to the house and cowered in front of the door. He thought Matt would be happy to see him. But instead, Chance was getting scolded. He didn't understand why Matt seemed so angry that he came home. Chance was scared and confused.

Never EVER scold a puppy when he comes to you. Even if you're disgusted with him, always reward him and act happy to see him when he returns. If you scold him or seem angry, he will learn to be afraid to come to you.

34

"Let's go in, Boomer," Andrew said, opening the back door. "I have to go away with Mom and Dad this afternoon. I'm sorry, Boy, but this time you can't come along." He walked into the house first, then held the door for Boomer.

Andrew stuffed a KONG with peanut butter. "You'll like this," he said. "Boomer, sit." Eager to get the treat, Boomer quickly obeyed. Immediately, Andrew gave him the toy. "Good sit," he said, giving him a pat.

Then Andrew filled the water bowl with fresh water and set it on the floor. He checked to make sure there were no electric cords within the puppy's reach, and looked around the kitchen for any other items that may be of danger to Boomer. Then he gated Boomer in the kitchen where he knew he would be safe.

While Boomer was still a puppy, Andrew never left him alone for more than a few hours at a time. When he had to be gone from home, he made sure that Boomer had first been taken outside to go potty. Then he gated him in the kitchen or outdoors in a shaded kennel, and made sure that fresh water was available.

Just before leaving, Andrew knelt down beside Boomer and petted his shiny, black coat. "Bye, Boomer," he said. "I'll be back."

If your puppy is busy chewing on a stuffed KONG (a hollow, tough rubber chew toy) or nylon bone when you are getting ready to leave, it will help him associate your leaving with a yummy-tasting treat. That, along with your quiet, cheerful "goodbye" can keep him happy, rather than getting stressed out about being left alone.

Some people prefer to crate their puppy while they are gone. Just remember that no puppy should be left alone for several hours.

"Mom, can't you *do* something about Chance!" growled Matt one morning. "He's chewed up my new shoes!"

"No, Matt, he's your dog. You're the one who promised to take care of him, remember? You figure it out. I don't know *anything* about puppies," she said, "but you better do something before he's chewed up all the shoes in the house!"

His mother sighed. "I don't know why I bothered buying those chew toys for that pup," she said. "All he does is tear them apart. I'm not wasting more money on something he's just going to destroy!"

Matt ran up the stairs and burst into his bedroom, yelling at Chance and waving a shoe at him. "Don't chew on my shoes!" he scolded. "Do you *understand*?!"

Chance woke up abruptly from his nap under the desk to find Matt standing over him, shaking a shoe in his face, and talking in a very angry voice.

Of course Chance *didn't* understand. He had no idea what Matt was talking about, and thought he must be in trouble for lying under the desk. Chance got out of there *fast* and never ever went under that desk again.

But he didn't stop chewing on shoes.

Puppies need to chew and they will chew.   It is better to spend a little money on chew toys now and then and to keep things you don't want ruined out of the puppy's reach.   A washcloth, soaked in water, then wrung out and kept in the freezer until you give it to him, makes a great chew toy for a puppy who's teething. Hollow bones or KONGs stuffed with food treats make good toys also and keep the puppy entertained.

If you come home from school and find that your puppy has eaten the entire bag of cookies you left next to your bed, don't scold him. Unless you catch him grabbing the bag of cookies, he will have no idea why you're upset with him.

Remember: it's your job to "puppy proof" your house.   It will keep your things from getting ruined, and it will protect your puppy.

42

One day that summer, as a storm approached, a long, low rumble of thunder could be heard. Boomer whined, ran to the living room, and tried to crawl under the sofa.

"Hey, Boomer, want to play ball?" called Andrew. He grabbed a tennis ball and rolled it toward the puppy, trying to get his mind off the storm. Boomer grabbed the ball with his mouth, jumped up, and ran to Andrew.

"Good boy, Boomer," Andrew said, taking the ball from him and tossing it again. In a minute, Boomer had forgotten all about being afraid.

Each time Boomer appeared timid, Andrew would use a happy tone of voice and try to distract him with a toy or a game. He always kept his voice confident.   In time, Boomer became confident too.

When a sudden flash of lightning lit up the sky, followed by a loud crack of thunder, Chance squealed and ran under the kitchen table to hide from the scary noise. Matt's mom knelt down, reaching under the table.

"It's okay, Chance," she said, in a soft and soothing voice, as she petted the frightened puppy. "It's okay."

Chance whimpered. He snuggled up beside Matt's mom, shaking timidly. She stayed beside him during the storm, petting him and trying to comfort him. She didn't realize it, of course, but she was showing Chance that it was okay to be scared. With each thunderstorm, he became more and more frightened.

If you fuss over your puppy when he is scared, it will only make things worse. Keeping a cheerful voice and distracting him with toys or games will go a long way toward helping your puppy develop confidence.

Boomer jumped up, standing on his hind legs, trying to get closer to Andrew's face.

"Off!" said Andrew in a firm voice. He turned away from Boomer, looked up at the sky, and ignored him until Boomer, once again, had all four feet on the ground.

"Good off, good off," said Andrew, getting down beside Boomer and petting him. He knew that puppies can learn bad habits quickly. Encouraging Boomer to jump up or play rough *even once* might make him think it was okay.

Matt ran outdoors with Chance following at his heels. "Let's play, Chance! Up! Up!" he said. Matt patted his chest with his hands, coaxing Chance to jump up on him.

Chance wiggled with excitement. He loved this game. He ran to Matt and jumped up, reaching as high as he could with his front paws.

Matt's friends would often join in too. They liked playing rough with Chance and teaching him to jump up.

One day, after a rain shower, Matt heard Grandma's car pulling up the driveway. "Grandma's here! Grandma's here!" he cried.

Chance loved Grandma and was always excited when she came to visit. As soon as Matt opened the door, Chance bolted out in front of him. He ran across the driveway, galloping through a mud puddle.

As soon as Grandma stepped from the car, Chance jumped up on her, causing her to lose her balance.

"Oh no!!" cried Grandma, as she tumbled to the ground. In a second, Chance was on top of her, muddy feet and all, wagging his tail and licking her face.

"Chance, no!" cried Matt, running after him. "Get off! Bad dog, bad dog!" Matt pushed Chance away and helped Grandma to her feet.

"I'm sorry, Grandma," he apologized. "I don't know *why* he does that." He swatted at Chance. "Bad dog!" he scolded. "You know better than that! Go lie down!"

"What is the matter with Chance?!" asked Grandma. "I'm glad he likes me, Matt," she said, "but this is ridiculous!" She picked up her bag and looked down at her jeans, now covered with muddy paw prints.

Matt stayed beside Grandma as she walked to the house. When he opened the door, Chance tried to barge in ahead of them. Matt shoved him aside.

"Forget it, Chance!" he said. "You're not coming in the house *now*!" Matt quickly slammed the door before the puppy could get in.

Chance whined and scratched at the back door. Eventually, he gave up, lay down on the porch, and sighed. He had thought that Matt liked it when he jumped up on people.

How is Chance supposed to learn good behavior? Sometimes Matt asks him to jump up, and sometimes he's angry with him for doing it. Chance is confused. He is not a bad dog. He is a good dog who needs good training. Matt and his friends don't realize it, but they are training Chance. They're training him to be rude.

At puppy kindergarten, Andrew had learned that he could use butter to help teach Boomer not to bite. Each day, he would rub a little butter on the palms of his hands. While Boomer was eagerly licking it off, Andrew would say, "Good kisses. Good kisses!"

Sometimes, when Andrew and Boomer were playing and Boomer started biting, Andrew would say, "Kisses. Kisses," and hold out his hand for Boomer to lick. That usually was enough to distract him.

Once in a while, though, if Boomer got really excited, that didn't work. As Boomer and Andrew were playing one day, the excited puppy grabbed Andrew's ankle with his sharp teeth.

"No!" Andrew scolded. "Kisses, Boomer, kisses," he reminded Boomer. This time, Boomer paid no attention to Andrew. He made a play bow, then lunged at Andrew, grabbing his ankle again.

"*Oooow!* That hurts!" cried Andrew, dropping to the ground and holding his ankle.

Startled, Boomer backed off for a minute, but soon he tried it again. "No!" cried Andrew, grabbing the puppy's muzzle and pushing Boomer's lips over those sharp little teeth. As Boomer continued biting, he was suddenly biting his own lips. That took him by surprise, and immediately, he stopped biting.

"Here, Boomer!" said Andrew, quickly distracting him with a toy that it was okay for him to bite. Soon Boomer was tearing the toy apart, pulling out the stuffing.

"That's right," said Andrew. "You chew on *that*, not on *me*!"

It took a lot of patience to teach Boomer about biting, but it paid off in the long run. As Boomer grew, Andrew was sure that his dog wouldn't get into trouble for biting anyone.

As Matt's mom took the pizza from the oven, she caught a glimpse of her nephew pestering Chance. "Tim," she begged, "leave that poor dog *alone*! You're asking for trouble."

Tim ignored her and continued to swing his hands in front of Chance's face, pretending to swat him. "C'mon, big fella," he teased. Suddenly, Chance nipped his hand. Tim shrieked and ran from the room. Chance was right behind him, nipping at his heels. By now, the rest of the family was laughing. As Tim began running up the stairs, Chance grabbed his pant leg, pulling him off his feet.

"Ow!" Tim screamed, collapsing on the steps. "Stop it! Stop it! No, Chance, no!!"

Matt's Mom ran to the steps. "Chance," she scolded, "go lie down!" Chance growled at Tim, then walked to the kitchen and curled up under the table.

A week later, Aunt Susan and little 18-month-old Sarah came to spend the afternoon. While Chance was resting in the corner, Sarah toddled up behind him, crouched down, and reached out to touch his tail. Chance whirled around and bit her.

"What is the *matter* with that dog!" cried Aunt Susan. *"Get him away from my baby!"* She snatched up the screaming little Sarah and tried to comfort her. No one thought that biting was funny *now*.

"Bad dog!" yelled Matt, as he grabbed Chance by the collar and dragged him outdoors. He clipped one end of a rope to the collar and tied the other end to the apple tree. Matt walked away. By the time he thought of Chance again, the poor pup had walked around the tree again and again, using up almost the entire length of rope. He couldn't move; he couldn't get to water.

Puppies can't be given mixed signals about behavior. Something is either okay or not okay, always. Even before a puppy has his adult teeth, a bite can be very serious. Puppies must be taught when they are young that jumping up on people or biting are never acceptable. Don't ever laugh at him for misbehaving. You will regret it. With a dog's sharp teeth and strong jaws, it is definitely not okay for them to get the wrong idea.

Remember: It is your job to make sure that anyone who spends time with your puppy understands and plays by the rules. Stand up for your puppy. Don't let other people tease him, mistreat him, or encourage bad behavior.

As Boomer grew up, Andrew enrolled him in more obedience-training classes. Teaching Boomer to obey commands wasn't to prove he was a smart puppy. Those commands would help keep Boomer safe.

Andrew also learned more about grooming Boomer, about taking care of his teeth, and many tips that would help him be a good caregiver for Boomer. Because Boomer had already been through puppy kindergarten, and was used to Andrew teaching him, it made obedience training a lot easier.

During dinner, Boomer would lie on the kitchen floor and wait for Andrew to finish eating. He didn't whine or beg for food, because no one had ever fed him from the table. After dinner, Andrew took him outdoors. Sometimes he would put a leash on Boomer and they would go for a walk. Other times they would play in the backyard, which was fenced in so Boomer would be safe.

In the evenings, Boomer would lie beside the desk as Andrew did his homework, or near the sofa as the family watched TV. At bedtime, Boomer would run up the stairs to Andrew's bedroom and curl up on his own fuzzy, soft bed. Boomer was a happy dog. He was definitely part of the family.

> *Obedience training takes time and effort. Andrew's parents helped reinforce Boomer's training by using the same commands that Andrew did. Good and consistent training will mean that you will have a happy dog and that other people will enjoy having him around.*

Matt got more complaints about Chance. The puppy always seemed to be in trouble for one thing or another. He chewed on shoes and boots, sofas and table legs. He got into *everything*, he snatched food from the counter, and sometimes he even nipped at people.

"Matt, you're going to have to keep Chance outside," said his dad one day. "It just isn't working out to have him in the house. He seems to ruin everything he can find, and some people are afraid of him. You're going to have to keep him tied up. You can let him loose and play with him when you get home from school in the afternoon."

"Well, Chance," said Matt, as he put the lead on the puppy and walked to the back yard, "It won't be so bad out here. I'll try to get a doghouse built soon. You'll be fine," he promised. "You'll get used to it."

As Matt turned to walk toward the house, Chance barked and lunged, trying to break free from the rope that tied him to the apple tree and kept him away from Matt.

Matt reached for the door, then took one look back at Chance. He opened the back door and walked into the house. Chance continued to lunge and bark. He could not get to his family no matter how hard he tried or how loudly he begged.

As time went by, Matt became busier with school and sports, and hardly ever took time to play with Chance. He petted him when he went out to give him water and food every day, but that was about all the attention Chance got. Most of Matt's friends had also lost interest in playing with the puppy. They seldom went over to pet him when they came to play.

Day after day, night after night, Chance spent his time eating, sleeping, and barking. The only thing he wanted was what he'd always wanted—to be part of the family.

"Matt, come here," said his father one day. Matt could tell by the tone of his voice that something serious was on his mind. "Matt, Chance does nothing but bark and dig up the yard.

Just look at that," he complained, pointing out the kitchen window. "We just can't have a dog around here. He wrecks *everything*."

He paused a moment, then slowly went on, his voice now almost a whisper. "Matt, I'm sorry, but you're going to have to get rid of Chance. Maybe the animal shelter can find a home for him. You *know* you don't have time for him anymore," he said.

Matt turned away, surprised to find tears welling in his eyes. But he didn't bother to argue.

"I guess you're right," he said, sadly. Things hadn't turned out the way he'd thought they would when he had brought home that cute, cuddly puppy a year ago.

Reluctantly, Matt got out the phone book and looked up the number of the animal shelter. Outside, tied to the apple tree, Chance had no idea that he was about to lose his home and his family.

Andrew lay on the living room floor, petting the happy dog that lay beside him. His mom looked at the two of them.

"I can hardly believe it's been over a year since we brought that cute little puppy home from the animal shelter," she said. "Look how much he's grown!"

Andrew smiled. He reached out to scratch Boomer behind the ears. Boomer stretched out, sighed, and closed his eyes, enjoying all the attention.

"You know, Mom," said Andrew, "I've been thinking about getting another puppy. I think it would be good for Boomer." The words rushed out. "There would be someone here to play with him when I have to be gone, so he'd never get lonely. Do you think I could, Mom?" he asked, now running out of breath.

"Whoa! Slow down, Andrew," she said, smiling at his enthusiasm. She didn't answer for a minute. Finally, slowly and thoughtfully, she said, "I'll have to admit, Andrew, that you've been very responsible about taking care of Boomer and training him. All your hard work has paid off. He's a wonderful dog. But do you remember what those first few weeks were like?" she asked, recalling the times that Andrew stood outside in the rain, waiting for Boomer to go potty.

"I know it's a lot of work, Mom, but I've done it before. I know I can do it again. I can handle the chores. I know I can," he said. "After all, I've been doing it for a long time, haven't I?" He waited for his mom to respond.

"Well, let's think this through a little longer," she said. "This weekend we can discuss it with your dad and make a decision."

"Okay," said Andrew. "I guess that's fair." The fact that his mom hadn't already said no was a pretty good sign. Andrew smiled. *She must not think that getting a puppy is such a bad idea!* he thought.

That weekend, after much discussion, the decision was made to get a puppy. They phoned the animal shelter where they'd found Boomer.

That afternoon, as Andrew walked into the large green building, he could hear little squeals and grunts coming from a new litter of puppies in the corner room. He looked at the little Labrador retrievers, snuggled against their mother.

Lying on the soft blankets, she stretched out and sighed as the puppies squirmed and pushed against her belly with their tiny paws, trying to get to their dinner.

Mr. Baker, a member of the staff, walked with Andrew and his mom to the outdoor pen and showed them another female—a German Shepherd—and her litter of five puppies who had been born eight weeks earlier. They were now old enough to leave their mother.

Andrew picked up a little black and brown puppy and cradled it in his arms. In the background, he could hear the sound of excited barking coming from a nearby building.

"Here you go, little fella," he said, setting the puppy down next to its littermates. "I'm gonna go check that out. I want to see what's going on over there."

Andrew went into the other building. As he walked slowly down the long row of kennels, he could hardly believe the number of homeless dogs he saw—terriers, herders, hunting dogs, working dogs—dogs all needing good homes.

When he turned the corner, Andrew was startled by what he saw. There, barking and pawing at the kennel was a dog who looked remarkably like Boomer.

Then Andrew noticed the sign above the door.

Andrew ran to find his mom. "You've got to come with me," he said, breathlessly, grabbing her by the hand. "I think I've found the right dog for us."

"What? But Andrew," she said, you're here to get a puppy, *remember*?"

"I know I was, Mom, but just wait 'til you see him!" he said.

Chance was standing on his hind legs, pawing at the kennel door and barking when Andrew and his mom walked into the room.

Andrew pointed at the sign. "Look, Mom," he said. "That dog has gotta be Boomer's brother."

"He looks a lot like him, doesn't he—and they're the same age, so I suppose he *could* be," she said, "but why would he be here? That doesn't make sense. I remember Mr. Baker told us there was another family coming to look at the puppies. I figured that puppy would be adopted the same day we got Boomer."

"Yeah, that's what I thought, too," said

Andrew. "I don't know what's going on. C'mon, Mom. Let's go see what we can find out about him. I bet Mr. Baker can tell us."

Mr. Baker walked across the office and sat down in front of the computer. "Well, let's see," he said, clicking on Chance's file and scanning the information. "You're right, Andrew," he said. "Chance is Boomer's littermate. He's the other puppy you saw the day you got Boomer."

He read further. "It says here that he barks, chews up everything, nips occasionally, and digs up the yard. This doesn't sound good." He glanced up at Andrew and his mom. "That's strange," he said. "He's been friendly to me, to the rest of the staff, and to the volunteers." Mr. Baker sadly shook his head. "Looks to me like no one bothered to give this dog the training he needed."

"Mom, I'd make sure he got training," said Andrew. "I would take him to obedience classes and I promise I wouldn't neglect Boomer. *I promise.*"

Andrew's mom smiled at the eager look on his face. "I think we'd better find out how Boomer feels about this," she suggested. "If he and Chance don't get along, it could be a disaster."

Andrew and his mom knew that it would be better for the two dogs to meet at the animal shelter, rather than suddenly showing up in Boomer's territory with a new dog. They drove home to get Boomer. When Andrew opened the car door for him, Boomer jumped onto the back seat. He had no idea where they were going, but he was always eager to get a ride in the car.

Mr. Baker put a lead on Chance and took him to the grassy yard where Andrew and his mom were waiting with Boomer. Immediately, Chance strained at the lead, wanting to get closer to

Boomer. The two dogs pranced toward each other with their heads up and their tails wagging.

As they stood next to each other, they first stiffened, then quietly studied and sniffed each other. Chance didn't seem aggressive, just curious and excited. Boomer didn't seem at all frightened, just interested and eager to make a new friend.

"I think it just might work, Andrew," said his mom, after watching the two dogs for a while. "If you promise to train Chance the way you've trained Boomer," she said, "then bringing him to our home would be a great thing for both him and Boomer."

"You know, Andrew," said Mr. Baker, "it's surprising how many people come here looking for a puppy. We have no trouble finding homes for puppies," he went on, "but it's not the same story once that puppy gets to be an adult." He looked at the two dogs who seemed to be getting along just fine. "I'm sure glad you made this decision, Andrew," he said. "I don't think you'll regret it."

Mr. Baker then knelt beside Chance. "Hey, fella," he whispered, stroking Chance's soft, shiny coat, "I wish every dog's story had a happy ending like this. You're going to a great home now. You're getting *two* new pals out of the deal. And I know Andrew—he'll take good care of you." He scratched the dog's hips, gave him a pat, then stood up. "Well," said Mr. Baker, smiling at Andrew and his mom, "maybe this dog should have been named 'Second Chance.'"

SUPPLIES FOR YOUR PUPPY

- **PUPPY FOOD:** (get your veterinarian's advice). Keep onions, chocolate, raisins, and grapes out of your puppy's reach. They are toxic to dogs.

- **2 STAINLESS STEEL BOWLS:** one for water; one for food.

- **BUCKLE COLLAR**

- **FOUR-FOOT LEAD:** for tethering your puppy to you during the housetraining stage.

- **A CRATE AND BLANKET:** for night time when your puppy is young.

- **SIX-FOOT LEAD:** for walking your puppy

- **BITTER APPLE SPRAY:** for those things that you can't keep out of your puppy's reach and he is determined to chew. If he begins to chew on his lead or the corner of the sofa, Bitter Apple sprayed on the item should discourage your puppy from chewing. Ask for Bitter Apple spray at your pet supply store.

- **DOG BED**

- **CHEW TOYS:** KONG, nylon bone, rope, stuffed toy, etc. Ask your veterinarian. Not all chew toys are safe for your puppy.

- **BALL:** one that is small enough for him to carry in his mouth, but large enough that he cannot choke on it.

NOTE TO PARENTS

Please share the following information with your child when considering getting a puppy or dog. Dogs are pack animals. When you take a puppy or dog into your home, your family is the pack to that animal. He needs to be near you, not left alone in the back yard.

Every year, millions of dogs are taken to animal shelters or dropped off in the country and abandoned. They are left to get run over, contract disease, or starve. Most animal shelters are not funded well enough to ensure that every dog will get to stay until a new home is found for him. It is estimated that over half of all animals entering shelters are euthanized.

A mis-trained dog, which seems a more appropriate term for it, rather than untrained, has a good chance of ending up dead. When dogs have developed bad behaviors, they are often unadoptable. The worst part is, the dog has no say in getting the training he needs. That depends upon you.

Don't get a puppy just because he is cute. Animal shelters are full of dogs who were once cute little puppies. Only get a puppy if you can and will make a commitment to train him. A dog who is well behaved is a delight to everyone. A dog who is welcomed as one of the family will prove his love and devotion for as long as he lives.

The story of Chance and Boomer is played out across the country every day. Puppies are taken home with little thought to their needs and their long-term care.

Before you get a puppy or dog, learn all you can about them. Libraries and bookstores contain many books on the subject. Determine the breed which best suits your family. If you're certain that you can and will give the puppy or dog the care he needs, only then should you take him into your home. Remember Boomer and Chance. Make a thoughtful decision. Your puppy's life will depend upon it.

SUGGESTED READING

Puppies for Dummies, Sarah Hodgson,
pub. IDG Books, 2000.

*Paws to Consider: Choosing the Right Dog for You
and Your Family*, by Brian Kilcommons,
pub. Warner Books, Inc.1999.

Smarter Than You Think, by Paul Loeb,
pub. Pocket Books, 1997.

The Other End of the Leash, by Patricia
McConnell Ph.D.pub. Ballantine Books, 2002.

The Art of Raising a Puppy, by the Monks of New
Skete, pub. Little, Brown and Company, 1991.

NOTES

INDEX

ABOUT THE AUTHOR

Judy Masrud lives in the rolling hills of northwest Wisconsin where she spends her time writing children's stories, gardening, and taking care of her two dogs. She lives with her husband, Kevin, and the three children who are still living at home. Her own experiences as a dog owner are the inspiration for the book *SECOND CHANCE, a Tale of Two Puppies.* Choosing a three-month old German Shepherd puppy for all the wrong reasons, she later took him to puppy kindergarten and then beginning obedience classes. Bridger was the only puppy in the group who had to have a "time out." Through the advice and instruction of the trainer, Judy learned that most of what she had been doing to try to train Bridger was having either the opposite effect or was simply ineffective. A year later, after visiting the local animal shelter to find a companion for Bridger, a lab-shepherd mix named Misty came to live with the Masruds. Seeing the many homeless dogs and puppies at the shelter, and realizing that so many of them were surrendered because of a lack of education on the part of their owners, Judy decided to write this book.

ABOUT THE ILLUSTRATOR

Cathy Pool lives in northwest Wisconsin in a beautiful lake city. She has done many portrait works in soft pastel, her favorite medium, and is currently working on wildlife paintings, including murals. Her favorite subjects are children and animals. Cathy lives with her three children, Ryan 12, Rene 11, and Nicole, 6. This is her first collaboration on a children's book.

www.birdseedbooksforkids.com

QUICK ORDER FORM

SECOND CHANCE—A Tale of Two Puppies: $9.95 ea.

Fax orders: 715-837-2041. Please fill out all information below.

Telephone Orders: 1-800-676-1160. Have your credit card ready.

Online Ordering: www.birdseedbooksforkids.com

Postal orders: Birdseed Books, 520 17th Street, Dallas, WI 54733

Please send me:

    _____copies of **SECOND CHANCE—A Tale of Two Puppies**

Please send me more information on: (please circle your choice):

- Quantity discounts on ***Second Chance—A Tale of Two Puppies*** (book clubs, classrooms, 4-H groups, animal shelters, rescue organizations, vet clinics, dog training classes, etc.)
- Ringbound Reading™ A colorful, hands-on, comprehensive phonics instruction curriculum for teaching reading. Gr. K-3

Name:_____

Address:_____

City:_____State:_____Zip:_____

E-mail address:_____

Sales Tax: Please add 5.5% for products shipped to Wisconsin addresses. Shipping & Handling $2.00 for first book, $1.00 each additional book.

Payment: (circle one):

- MasterCard
- Visa
- Check

Card number: _____

Name on card:_____Exp. Date:_____

THANK YOU!